A FINE CAULDRON OF FISH

CORNELIA AMIRI

PREFACE

On the Isle of Man, you can find the vampiric fey known as the lhiannan shee, dwelling in sea caves where they keep a red cauldron filled with the blood of their human lovers. Mortal men cannot resist them, they enchant and enslave them with their beauty alone.

INTRODUCTION

A fairy tale romance as hot as summer itself.

Hi, I'm Andrew, vacationing on the mystical Isle of Man.
    Looking for summer fun—sun, sea, and hot girls.
    So, I hit the jackpot,
    when I meet a dreamy, seductive babe.

    There're only a couple of minor problems:
    Margaid lives in a cave under the sea,
    is invisible,
    and thinks drinking my blood,
    will save her from turning into a water horse!

But hey, whoever said love was perfect!?

    In this secret fey world,
    where passion meets peril,
    can our love conquer all,
    or will the waves of fate pull us apart forever?

Editorial Reviews:

"A Fine Cauldron of Fish is a very funny story of gods and sidhe on the Isle of Man. This is just a quick, fun read and one I highly recommend." Reviewer Chere Gruver of Paranormal Romance

"What do you get when two clumsy people get together an outright laugh-a-minute comedy in A Fine Cauldron of Fish." Reviewer by Cheryl Koch of Cheryls Book Nook

"A Fine Cauldron of Fish is hilarious. I laughed out loud several times through this story. If you like things a bit out of the ordinary and are in the mood for a fun light-heart read, then I recommend this." Reviewer Vee at Night Owl Romance Book Reviews

A Fine Cauldron of Fish©2013 by Cornelia Amiri

This is a revised edition of Cornelia Amiri's

A Fine Cauldron of Fish,

Previously published in 2008 by Eternal Press

This book is a work of fiction. Characters, names, places, and incidents are either the product of the author's imagination or are used fictionally, and any resemblance to any actual persons, living or dead, events, or locales is entirely coincidental.

CHAPTER 1

Ready to pounce on the first virile man she spotted, Margaid tread water near a docked boat. With the salty taste of the sea on her tongue, she drew in a deep gulp of air. Wet hair whipped her shoulders as she shook her head in anger, still seething about the sea god's threat.

"You are the only one of the lhiannan shee who gives me problems. All the others use their beauty to lure and seduce men then drain their blood into red cauldrons," she imitated Mannan beg mac y Leir in a clownish voice.

Margaid swept her long red hair back from her freckled face. Maybe he was right. She deserved to be turned into a water horse for not being a good lhiannan shee—for all these centuries, never once doing what the lhiannan shee were supposed to do.

The muscles in her neck clinched like a knot tugged tight. She didn't like blood. It was too red and smelly and yuck—bloody.

Her attention shifted to one of the poles supporting the dock. With the gentle sway of the waves, water rose and fell against the wood, moving up and down the thick pole, again and again. The muscles in her abdomen pulled tight and her breath grew shallow. She was hot. "From spending too much time alone," she said aloud. She needed a hard, muscular man in her cave on the seabed. Have some fun with the human before she filled her cauldron with his blood.

The red orb in the sky hung over Douglas Bay as it set. Margaid peered at a grand building, lit up like gold. She'd heard people call it things like 'the Hilton' and 'the casino.' As a man walked out of the building, she smiled, gazing at his hair, the color of the yellow sponge plants that clung to the boulders by the entrance of her underwater cave. His only imperfection was a cowlick, which stuck out like the feathers on a crested bird.

Margaid swam here to find a man. Now she'd spotted one. She glided through the water toward him. As she approached, she noticed he squinted his eyes, which made him look rather funny. It also eased the shakiness inside her.

"*Laa mie*," she greeted him in her most tempting tone.

He stepped to the edge of the dock where she tread water. "Hi."

"Come join me, the water's fine." Why is he still squinting? It's nighttime, so it's not because of the sun's glare. "Jump in for a swim."

"I don't have my swim trunks." He leaned his head to the side and pressed his lips together. "My luggage got lost."

"Did you look for it?"

His throaty chuckle danced in the air. "No, the airline lost it. My contacts were in it."

"Your contacts? People you know?"

"You're funny." His mouth spread into a dimpled smile, though he still squinted his eyes. "No, for my eyes, like glasses but better." He shrugged. "My eyes irritated me, so to be comfortable on the flight, I took out my contacts and stuffed them in a carry-on bag before we boarded. But my mom had two carry-on satchels and her purse, so they shoved mine in the baggage compartment, where they lost it." He smiled. "They should find it soon."

"You came in an airplane." Perfect, a stranger from far away. "I've seen them fly over the sea."

"Yeah, I'm from America."

"America? Is it a large island, like Man?"

"No, much larger." There was a trace of laughter in his voice. "And it's not an island." Pausing, he tapped his finger against his chin. "Oh, you probably call it the United States."

"I've never met anyone who didn't live on an island." She flashed her brightest smile at him. "So, you've come to live here on Man instead of America?"

"No, we're on vacation." He hesitated. "Well, my mother and brother came to discover their roots, but I came for fun. I stumbled from the hotel club to see what else was out here."

She bobbed her head in agreement. "I also come to the island at night to look at what's out here."

"Anything going down tonight, do you know the spot to go to?"

"Yes, I'll take you there, jump in." She curled her fingers and gestured to him.

"In the water?"

"Yes, under the sea."

Laughter flowed from deep in his throat.

"You don't need a swimsuit." In response to his contagious chuckles, her giggles rippled through the air. "Slip off your shoes and dive in."

"Why not?" He kicked off his shoes. "Is that a bikini you're wearing?"

"No, a chiton. It's easy to swim in."

"Oh, I know it's short and sleeveless. Other than that, it's hard to see without my contacts." He shed his black t-shirt with the graphic of a helmeted rider, tagged 'Isle of Man, Road Racing Capital of the World.'

Margaid's eyes locked on his rock-solid chest, the flat, dusky nipples, the smooth flesh of his defined abdomen ripped into six sections, and the dip of his belly button in the center of his firm, taut stomach. Her palms itched to touch and caress his muscular body. Her eyes drifted to his jeans and the large bulge between his thighs, which proved she aroused him as much as he stirred her desire.

"Shouldn't you take your pants off before you jump in?" Even in the cold water she felt hot, her heart raced, and she had trouble catching her breath.

"Can't." His eyes held a devilish gleam as he flashed a dimpled grin. "I'm going commando."

With his jeans on, he dove in headfirst, then shot up for air with a short yell. "Crazy! The water's like ice."

"It's warm to me." She had to get this man to her lair, or she'd be turned into a water horse for sure. "You'll get used to it. Come on, follow me." Ducking underwater, she swam away, hoping he'd chase her.

Through blue swirls of water dotted with tiny bubbles, she kept her pace slow so he could keep up. Forcing herself not to look back and appear over-eager, she glided on, hoping he still followed. She could be a proper lhiannan shee. She could do it.

She swam back to Andrew. As he treads water, his head and chest peaked out above the surface of the sea. His wet flesh looked so slick she had to touch him, had to see if his skin felt smother than the porpoise she'd recently petted. She stretched out her hand and tapped the tips of her fingers on his firm, chiseled chest.

"What?" He glanced at his chest.

"Nothing. A bit of seaweed clung there," she lied. "It's gone now."

She had to fight a riveting desire to wrap her arms around him, cling to him like seaweed and press her breast against his chest. Her nipples tightened at just the thought of such a sultry embrace.

"Did you see that porpoise?" His eyes grew wide, and his smile stretched across his whole face. "I've never been that close to one before."

"Yes, they swim all around here. We're almost at my house." She took his arm in hers. "Come." She dunked underwater with him and swam at his side.

Andrew didn't know it, but Margaid used her magic to allow him to share her ability to hold her breath much longer than humanly possible. He could never free dive this long or this deep on his own.

They passed a large leatherback sea turtle flapping its rough front and back flippers as its narrow head bobbed in the water. As they dived deeper, Andrew pointed to stingrays with hooded eyes that sailed passed, flapping wide, dark wings as their serpentine tails swayed in a titillating fashion. The whip-like tails all bore long spines at the tip, able to penetrate deep into soft, sensitive flesh. Margaid pointed to a conger eel hiding under a nearby rock, sticking out its large, thick head. Its two black eyes stared at Margaid accusingly, as if it knew what she was about to do. The big eel's long spindle shaped body slithered over the boulders towards the entrance to her cave.

Andrew drew back, but she dragged him forward until

their feet hit the soft sand at the seabed. Who was that eel to judge who she chose to take to her cave? What could she do, either be a proper lhiannan shee or be a water horse. She had no choice.

Holding Andrew's hand in hers, Margaid stood in front of a boulder engraved with ancient Celtic swirls forming a triskelion, the symbol of Mannan beg mac y Leir. Shoving the boulder aside, she stepped through the entrance onto the stairs, which led into the cave. With Andrew inside, she shut the hatch.

———

"Wow, I can breathe here. Just like on land." Andrew followed her down. "Man, this is crazy. You really live under the sea. I thought you were joking." He took the last step off the stairs and pressed his hands on her shoulders, resting them there in a lingering touch that was firm yet gentle.

She'd noticed earlier that his fingers were long, and his wrists thick, in fact everything about Andrew seemed so manly. She peered at his wet jeans, which clung to his firm ass and his athletic legs.

Margaid turned her gaze to her humble abode, wondering how it would compare to his own house. She glanced at the ceiling and the two favorite features of her cozy cave. First, the cluster of long rock-sickles dangling above her dining area. A burning beeswax candle mounted on each stalactite transformed it into a grand, yet natural chandelier. The second one was above her living room, a round glass pane which looked out on the blue-violet sea, where rainbow-hued fish swam by, shimmering with light from their glossy scales.

She noticed Andrew's gaze swept over the rock walls of

the cavern and settled on the ancient tapestry of white embroidery on a maroon background depicting a flat boat full of men. A border of Celtic knot work surrounded the ship.

He crossed the sand-packed floor to an antique wooden sofa and plopped down on the thin, green cushion.

"Not bad." Andrew's gaze lingered the longest on an ivory- hued stalagmite, which resembled a spiral mountain with a forest of cone trees sprouting up its side. "Did you steal this one from a museum?"

"Oh, you mean it looks like modern art?" Margaid sat down on the sofa beside him.

"I'm glad you like it." She pointed to the ceiling. "The sea made it over time, drip by drip." *Why do I care what he thinks? After all, I have to kill him. By the sword of Mannan beg mac y Leir, I'm not ready for this.*

As he laughed, he leaned his body toward her.

She inhaled Andrew's briny scent of the sea mixed with a rich, musky aroma. The energy and heat rolling off him struck her like a heavy wind. She wet her lips as she gazed at his full lips, hungering for a kiss. She tilted her head until their mouths touched, and she pressed hers hard against his, still wet and salty from the sea. When his lips parted, she thrust her tongue into his mouth, swirling it around the roof. A stream of fire coursed through her. Andrew released a low moan.

His mouth tasted like fresh mint. As he cupped her shoulders and pulled her closer, his tongue tangled with hers. Hardly able to breathe, she was lightheaded, woozy from his kiss.

As he dragged his lips off hers, he peered into her eyes. Though he squinted. "I wish I could get a better look at you."

"You see me, right?" Her beauty alone should seduce him, that's what Mannan had told her. Though more kissing sounded like a good idea.

"What I can see, I like."

"Good." She licked her lips, which still burned from his kiss. "I like what I see too."

She wrapped her arms around the warm, firm flesh of his broad shoulders and tilted her neck until her lips hovered over his. Her inner abdomen muscles drew tight, and she was so hot with need. Margaid flicked her tongue out and ran it along his soft lips, tracing them. Andrew grasped her waist with his hands, bracing her as his lips crushed hers.

Her heart pounded from the tight pressure between her thighs and the taste of salt and mint from his mouth. She eased her lips from his and tried to gather her thoughts as she took in a deep breath.

His mouth spread into a wide, flirtatious smile. Just when she'd caught her breath, he pointed at the red cauldron. "What's that in the middle of the floor?" Andrew squinted again. "It looks like a large pot."

"It's a lhiannan shee cauldron, you know, it's fey."

"Fey?" He stood and walked over to it. "It's huge, as large as a table."

"It's not for mortals." She shrugged. "Well, it is, partly." She rubbed her upper teeth over her lower lip. "You know what a lhiannan shee is, right?"

"No." He flashed a broad toothy grin.

Her stomach and lower muscles clinched tight at his smile. She licked her lips, hungry for another kiss. "It's because you're from America." She swept her wet hair back behind her ear. "Lhiannan shee only live on the Isle of Man."

"Never heard of them." One golden eyebrow arched. "Are they like the illuminati or skull and bones?"

"No, they're...oh, it doesn't matter." Her gaze fixed on his gleaming eyes, at least he wasn't squinting. "You said your mother's searching for her family roots in Man."

"Yes, the Quayles."

"I know that name. Seafarers from ancient times. They use to honor Mannan beg mac y Leir each Midsummer's Eve. They'd carry meadow grass to the top of Barule Mountain for the god and ask him to bless the boats and give them a good catch for the year."

"Yeah, people believed all that stuff long ago, but now days everyone knows none of it's real."

She gasped. "Mannan is quite real."

"You believe in this sea god, do you?"

"He's part of my life. You could say he's my father."

The contagious sound of Andrew's laughter rippled through the underwater cavern.

She chuckled with him.

Then she gave him her most seductive look by parting her

lips slightly and fluttering her lashes. "Let's talk about something more interesting than an old god." She grasped the scooped neckline of her chiton and slid it down to expose the top of her breasts.

After gaping at her bosom for some time, his eyes were reddened and his squint more severe. "Man, I need my contacts."

"Contacts?" She touched the side of his face. The slight stubble tickled her fingers as she slid them down his cheek then curled them under his chin. "No, it's me you need." Grasping his firm chin, she pulled his faced closer to hers.

His cheeks flushed red. "Yes."

Gazing deep into his blue eyes, she slid her fingers off his chin and stood. Facing him in her wet chiton, which clung to her body, she cupped her breasts with both hands, squeezing and stroking them. Her entire body tingled.

She slid her hands to her shoulders. Fumbling with the broaches pinning the fabric, she managed to unfasten them. The draped cloth fell free, baring her breasts to his gaze. She set the brooches on the old sea chest in front of the sofa.

"Beautiful." His whiskey tone and the hungry look in his eyes sent a jolt of heat through her.

She slipped her fingers through the braided hemp belt tied at her waist and swayed her hips from side to side. She had to seduce him or she'd never be able to kill him.

This was not what she wanted. Still, she didn't want to be a water horse either. She slid her fingers up to the knot and worked it loose. Margaid pulled the belt free and the fabric that clothed her but a moment ago fell into a puddle of cloth at her feet. She stepped out of it and kicked it aside toward an ancient clay pot stuffed with bright, cheery coral. This was it. There was no turning back now. He was hers.

She stood fully nude before him, grasping the braided rope belt in her hands. No reason why she couldn't have a little fun before the whole drain his blood into the cauldron thing.

As he squinted at her breasts, she twisted the hemp belt into a handcuff tie. "Stand up."

He did so.

She peered deep into his eyes, as blue as the summer sky above the Irish Sea when it mesmerizingly serene. She held the rope out. "Slip your hands in here."

Without hesitation, he did so. She drew the knot tight, binding his hands.

"Hey, what?"

"You're mine." She grasped his jeans at the waist, undid the button, and slid the zipper down. "I can touch you, but you can't touch me."

Andrew swallowed hard and rasped, "Hey, whatever you say."

She knelt before him and slid his jeans down his muscular legs to pool at his ankles. With his hands tied and his feet caught loosely in his pants, he was at her mercy, and she loved it. Of course, he had no idea of the danger she truly held for him. Andrew was much more of a captive than he knew.

She tilted her head, and with the bright light of the burning candles in the stalactite chandelier and in the iron sconces mounted on the cave walls, she explored his body with her eyes. Her gaze settled on the bulge of manly flesh bobbing before her.

Margaid reached out and ran her finger down his long cock. She wrapped her hand around the smooth base, slid her tongue over the knob, then licked his entire erection up and down. The taste of salt from his skin lingered on her tongue. Andrew moaned. She opened her mouth and wrapped it around his thick cock. She released her hold on his shaft to grasp his hips with both her hands to brace herself as he arched his hips forward, then rocked back, gliding his cock in and out of her mouth. With each of his thrusts, she sucked deeper. As her mouth stretched around his girth, he grew harder and larger.

"Your mouth is so hot," Andrew moaned.

The seduction was going well so far. Margaid pulled her mouth off him. She pushed to her feet and untied his hands. But once she drained his blood, she'd never be able to have fun with him like this again.

He stepped out of the pants, puddled at his feet, and kicked them aside. "You're wonderful."

She winced, then forced a smile for him as if nothing was wrong. "Are you having fun?" She didn't want to kill the delectable human. Still, she had to.

As she held the rope belt loosely in one hand, Andrew swooped her into his arms and captured her lips in his. He twisted his wet lips against hers.

A path of fire blazed through her veins. Her pulse pounded. Isn't it supposed to be the other way around? He's supposed to lose his control so I can drain his blood.

Torrid heat spread through her hands as they roamed the plane of his broad back.

Each time she stepped forward, he took a step back, as if she led him in a dance. Until she shoved him back against the cauldron, which stood waist-level to him.

With a hot, tingling sensation in her fingers, her nails extend into talons. She took a deep breath. All she had to do was claw his bare back and shed his blood. Margaid turned her head. She couldn't look at him while she killed him.

Her gaze fell onto the wall behind the cauldron, onto a tapestry bursting with hand-stitched trees and flowers, except for the center, where a trio of men in tunics and trouser hose were depicted with their greyhounds. She wondered again what it would be like to live on land with bright red, yellow and purple blossoms, towering green leafed trees and the mix of sweet and invigorating scents. Maybe she could live there with Andrew. If only there was a way. With those gentle, dreamy thoughts, her talons transformed back into fingernails.

She felt the rope belt slide out of her hand. She glanced down. He held it now. Before she could step back, he grabbed her arms, pressed them together, and wound the rope around her wrists.

He pulled the hemp rope into a tight knot.

"What are you doing?" She had to have her hands free for her nails to extend into talons again so she could draw his blood.

"The safe word is red if you want to stop." Andrew scooped her into his arms, and cradling her, he carried her to the wall.

He set her on her feet, grabbed her tied wrists, raised them above her head, and held them against the wall. With his other hand, he flicked the nipple on one breast and bent his head, taking an erect peak in his mouth. Then he slid his hand between her thighs and slipped his fingers through the folds. She gasped and mewed. All thoughts fled her mind as a fiery sensation filled her.

He slipped a finger inside her. "You're so wet, so tight."

Her shallow breath fell into a heavy pant. He pulled his finger out and spread her legs apart with his hand.

"I want you so bad." He guided his cock into her. He thrust, filling her completely.

She gasped with his sudden, powerful entry. He drew almost all the way out then sunk into her, pounding her hard.

Her mind felt foggy. She drew in short breaths. "So good."

"I wish I could see you better." He slid his mouth down to her breast and clamped his lips onto her nipple.

Fire surged in her veins. Margaid's heart hammered. His mouth felt hot upon her skin as he suckled her breast.

He hammered her, thrusting higher and deeper. "You like that?"

"Yes, oh yes." I can't kill him. Not when he makes me feel like this. "I'm so glad I decided to seduce you."

"I thought I was seducing you." Andrew spasmed against her, his breath came in a hard rush.

Margaid's pulse fluttered wildly. Her moist inner walls clenched hard, and her body shuddered. She'd seduced him like she was supposed to. Although she knew this wasn't what the sea god had in mind.

With each fast gasp of breath, she let out a shriek of ecstasy. Margaid was engulfed by the sensation of fire shooting through her as if she was the volcano on the Isle of Man in full eruption. Just when she felt fully spent, Andrew's body went still. He pulled out of her.

"Can you untie my hands now?" She could hear the strain and breathiness in her voice.

He undid the knot, and she tossed the rope belt onto the floor.

Once again, she had her chance to save herself from transformation into a water horse. As she leaned into his sweat covered body, her breasts tingled, pressing against his chest.

She was a lhiannan shee. They seduced men, drained them of blood, and filled their red cauldrons with it. That was who she was, and that was what she had to do. She had no choice, kill him, or spend the rest of her life as a water horse.

With her body molded to his, she stepped forward, leading him backwards, toward the cauldron. Finally, she had him where she needed him.

It is who I am, what I do. But what of his mother with the two carry-ons? She won't have her son or his luggage. No, no, I must. I cannot let Mannan beg mac y Leir down again. Perfect. I'm ready.

She leaned tighter against his body, but before she could transform her nails and raise her hands to attack him, he tumbled backwards into the cauldron. Lying on his back at the bottom of the great pot, his two legs dangled in the air.

She couldn't help but laugh.

"I'm glad this was empty. What do you usually keep in here, anyway?"

"Usually nothing. I'm supposed to keep blood in it."

"Oh...I know that's a joke, but I don't really get it." The large iron cauldron caused his voice to echo.

She grabbed his hand and pulled him up and out of the giant pot.

"Don't worry. I'm not going to get you." When his face screwed into a confused expression, she added, "I mean, I don't think you should die. I can't go through with it."

"I thought you just did go through with it." He laughed. "I'm not sure what you're talking about, but I don't plan on dying anytime soon."

"I don't plan on it either, though I'll probably be turned into a *cabyll-ushtey*."

"I don't think what we were doing will turn you into whatever you said."

"It will. Mannan beg mac y Leir won't abide me any longer. I'm a bad lhiannan shee."

"Is that like a bad girl?"

"It's a lhiannan shee that can't seduce a man and drain his blood, like I'm supposed to."

He drew back from her. "You're getting weird."

"I don't think you should die without your luggage or your contacts. You should be able to at least see what's around you in the last moments of your life. Don't you think so?"

"Yes," he said with a sideways glance.

Plus, I like you too much to kill you. "But Mannan beg mac y Leir won't agree with that. I'm supposed to do what a lhiannan shee does. Yet, I don't. I can't. I really tried this time. I am a failure as a lhiannan shee, so I'll soon be a *cabyll-ushtey* instead."

"What is a *cabyll-ushtey* and what are you talking about?

"Oh, another type of fey. They look like a horse, and they swim in the sea. I'm talking about this." She held up her hand to show him how her nails had transformed when she was ready to take his blood.

He screamed and jumped back. "Those are claws, and they look sharper than my pocketknife. Someone at the club must have spiked my drink with something that's making me crazy."

"No, they're real. You're in an underwater cave beneath the sea with a large red cauldron in it. What did you think this was all about? If you lived on the Isle of Man, you would know about the lhiannan shee and Mannan beg mac y Leir."

"Gods and underwater vampire women aren't real, just myths. If you believe any of this, you're insane."

"No Andrew, you can see it all yourself. Look, my nails are changing back since I'm not draining your blood." Holding her hands up, she watched as her nails returned to their normal length. "See?" She pointed to the pot. "That is the red cauldron of a lhiannan shee. We fill them with the blood of our victims. We wander the Isle of Man at night to find men, seduce them, bring them to our underwater cave and fill the red cauldron with their blood."

"So you're going to kill me."

"No, it's too late. When we cannot seduce and drain a man of blood, we become his slave. You are my master now.

I must serve you until you die, then Mannan beg mac y Leir will most likely turn me into a *cabyll-ushtey*."

"No, no." He rocked his head, like a silver pendulum ball. "See, I'm an American. I can't have a slave." He glanced toward the stairs leading out of her cave. "People go to jail over stuff like that."

"You mean you don't even want me as a slave?"

"All I want right now is to get out of here." He ran to the stairs.

"It doesn't matter where you go. I'm enslaved to you now. I'll instantly appear wherever you are, though only you can see me."

"This can't be real. I've had fun, but it's time to go." He rushed up the steps, forced the hatch open, shoved the boulder aside, and swam from the bottom of the sea back to shore.

CHAPTER 2

Every time he glanced back, he saw Margay behind him. The freaky woman meant to kill him with her nails, but that couldn't be true. He must have imagined it. And this slave stuff, the last thing he needed was a Manx woman following him around saying he was her master. That would cause all kinds of trouble.

Why did he always get mixed up with crazy girls? He didn't even know what Margay really looked like. Damn, he needed his contacts.

The water cut through his skin like ice and Andrew trembled when he climbed onto shore.

Margay pulled herself out of the water. She tilted her head to the side and shrugged. "I told you, I'm still here."

"Go away."

He'd just wanted a little fun. Party with a mutual one night fuck buddy. He' d heard of this sort of thing happening to girls, after a one night stand the guy would stalk them, but he didn't know it happened to men. Why him? He had to be the one guy who went on vacation and partied with a stalker freak.

"Andrew, I can't leave you, I'm your slave no matter what. It's not my choice."

"You can't follow me around. And don't tell anyone you're my slave. Now get away from me."

Mentally insane women weren't part of his vacation plans. Even though her skin was the softest he'd ever felt, her luscious breasts overflowed from his hands when he cupped them, and when he sheathed her, how sweet, the perfect fit, so tight and wet. His cock twitched at the thought. Hard already, apparently his treacherous dick didn't care if the girl was a nut, but his mind did. After all, some part of his body had to look out for him.

Coo coo was not good. Sure, the girls-gone-wild kind of crazy was all right, but not the drain-your-blood kind. That was a whole different set of crazy. Not what he needed in a girlfriend.

"I can't leave. It's fey lore, there are rules. Think about how you swam to and from the bottom of the sea without breathing. You did it because of fey magic. Just like the cows, the pigs, even the children the fey steal are taken Underhill, places mortal creatures shouldn't be able to live." She raised her hands to the side of her face, they trembled with frustration. "When a fey creature wants a mortal to come with them, the human accompanies them by the rules of fey lore, which override the laws of nature." Her features tightened like she was about to cry. "I wouldn't make this up. I'm your slave because when you tied my hands it interrupted my seduction, what I was supposed to do. It's the same as if you resisted my charms. So, by fey law, I'm your slave. I can't change it. I go where you go, no matter what." She rubbed the side of her head with her hand and her plump, wet lips formed a scowl.

He had to get rid of her. What kind of person lived in a

cave at the bottom of the sea? The girl was clearly off her rocker, thinking she had to fill a giant cauldron with his blood. She hears the god Mannan, telling her he's going to turn her into a water horse.

Still, no woman had ever made him feel like she did. Even now just seeing her, his cock hardened and swelled. "Look, you're not making any sense. You've got to be schizo." That's it. Schizophrenia's a disease. "You're confused, and that's not my fault." Hospitals, mental wards, that's where people like her go. "Margaid, if you want to come with me, you can. I just have to make a stop before I go back to the hotel."

He'd like to take her to the hotel, sleep with her again, but she was too batty. He'd passed a hospital when he left the club. They would help her, hold her. "I wish I could get out of these wet clothes first. They're kind of hard to explain."

Glancing back, he saw Margaid walk up to a man standing alone. She reached up and pulled the guy's shirt off him.

Andrew ran to her. "Stop it!"

"No!" The shirtless man turned to him. "You have the wrong idea. It's not me. I'm not doing it. Something's happening to me!" His face was red with embarrassment and his eyes were large with shock.

"No, of course it's not you. It's her." Andrew pointed at the lhiannan shee. "Don't, stop it." Andrew grabbed her arm as she held the poor guy's shirt. "You can't run up to a strange man and start taking off his clothes."

Before Margaid could answer, the guy shook his head at Andrew. "It's okay. You can keep my shirt. Although I don't know how you're holding it when your arm's about four inches away from it, but hey, I'm sure I simply had too much to drink. Keep it, that's fine."

"What? No, I don't want your shirt. Margaid, well she thought I wanted it, but–"

"No, don't let him go." Margaid shook her head. "You do want his shirt. And you need his pants, too."

Before Andrew knew what was happening, she shoved the shirt into his arms. Then she turned back to the quaking man and grabbed hold of his waist.

"Oh, no, don't do it." The moment Andrew yelled out, he knew she wasn't going to listen.

Andrew watched in utter horror as Margaid unsnapped the poor man's jeans, yanked down his zipper, and slid his pants all the way to his ankles.

"Damn, I'm glad he's wearing underwear." Black boxers with writing all over them. "What does that say?" Andrew read aloud, "B is for big."

"You don't say?" Margaid flashed a sheepish grin at the fairly respectable bulge underneath the man's boxers.

Andrew held his palm up in a stop gesture. "I'm warning you, don't touch his underwear."

"But don't you need a dry pair?"

Andrew shook his head. "I don't wear them."

The man gasped. Fear glittered in his eyes. "Please don't touch me. You can have my clothes. Okay?"

"I don't want your clothes. I'm not going to hurt you or touch you. Margaid misunderstood. She's not quite right." Andrew whipped his head toward her. "Give him his clothes."

"No, no, it's okay. I don't know what's going on here. But I'm going to leave. Keep the clothes." The man bolted down the street at a breakneck pace.

"You're lucky he didn't call the cops on you." He shook his head at Margaid.

"He's not going to call the police on me." She cupped the side of her face. "He might on you."

"What? You sound like him. He blamed me instead of you. He let you take his clothes off him just because you're a woman."

"That's not it." Her tone was curt, as if she was losing her patience. "He can't see or hear me. No one can, except you, because I'm your slave."

"That's nuts. I can't believe you stole the guy's clothes."

She leaned her head down and rubbed her forehead. "I thought you needed them."

"No, not like that." She looked so downcast and confused. "Look, it's okay, don't cry." He pointed to the jeans Margaid still held.

"He's gone, so I might as well put those on. At least you didn't take his B is for Big shorts." As crazy as the whole thing was, Andrew couldn't help but laugh. "He can keep those."

Margaid chortled along with him. "I wonder if he can live up to the claim."

"I'm glad you didn't insist on finding out."

"I'm your slave now. I follow your commands. When you say stop, I have to stop."

"Really? I recall having to yell stop several times before you actually did."

"Well, my obey-my-master skills may be a little rusty."

"Oh, a little." Despite the fact that he didn't believe anything she told him, he was having a lot of fun with this girl. "How many masters have you had?"

"You are the first."

"Ah, so you were able to seduce your other victims with no problem."

"No, in my whole life, I never tried to seduce a man and drain his blood before. You're my first human. All my male friends have been fey."

"Oh, and you saw me and thought it would be fine to drain my blood?"

"No, what made me finally try to do what my kind are supposed to do, was Mannan beg mac y Leir's threats to turn me into a water horse. So, I went hunting for a victim. Once I spotted you, with golden sun-kissed hair framing such a kissable face, an impressive height and build hinting of sculptured muscles fluidly moving beneath your clothing, I couldn't look at anyone else. That's why I picked you."

"When you put it that way, it almost sounds flattering. But can this Mannan really change you into some creature?"

"Oh yes. He is skilled at changing people, and himself, into other things. He's the god of transformation."

"I thought he was the god of the sea."

"He's the god of transformation, the sea god, and the trickster god."

"I should have known he was a trickster god based on what I've heard of him so far."

After a quick intake of breath, Margaid warned, "You must not criticize the gods. It's not wise. Not at all."

"Well, this is the guy or god who wanted you to drain my blood, I'm sure I'm entitled to make a negative comment or two about him." Andrew let out a sigh. "That was strange, though. That poor guy you stripped blamed me as if he really couldn't see you."

"He couldn't."

"No, no, it's like he said, he was just so drunk."

"You think so?"

"Yes, did you notice his tattoos?" He couldn't help but notice the Celtic symbols. One was an eye shaped like a fish with a fishtail on the end. "They were bad ass."

"No, I didn't see them, I was too busy taking his clothes off."

Andrew noticed the building across the street. "Come here." He led Margaid there and to the alley behind it. "Let me try these on. Turn around."

She did as he asked, shed his wet jeans, and pulled on the naked man's pants and blue polo shirt. "That's better, I'm all dry now. But what about you? Your dress is soaked."

"Don't worry about me. I don't mind, I like water. And no one can see me but you. So it doesn't matter." She was staring at his crotch. "Are those that man's pants?"

"Yeah, the ones you stole right off him." He'd get her to the hospital, and they would get her dry clothes there, a gown are something. She needed help. What else could he do but take her there?

"They fit differently on you."

"How? What's wrong?" He looked down to see what she meant.

"Oh, nothing's wrong. They seem a little tighter in the right place, that's all."

Staring at his hard on, she had that funny expression again, but he didn't mind. Not at all. Andrew grinned as his cock stiffened and enlarged even more, just from her gaze. He wished he had his contacts so he could see exactly what she looked like.

Maybe he could take her to the hotel. Spend his vacation with her. Her breasts were so lush and round. Even with his bad eyesight, he could see that. And her skin so soft. It had been heaven to be inside her, but no, that wasn't right. She needed help. He cleared his throat. "Right. I'm going to help you get help. The nurses at the hospital will get you into a clean, dry gown. Then the doctors will help you see you're not invisible. And I'll come and check on you before my vacation's over. Come on. I have an important errand I need to run."

He led her down the street until he came to a stop in front of a modern style, two story, light-colored brick building. The large sign out front read Nobles Hospital. "Here we are. They'll help you."

She shrugged. "Help me with what?"

———

He took her in through the emergency entrance and up to the window where a lady intake clerk in blue scrubs greeted them.

"Andrew, they're going to help me do what?"

"Just a moment." Holding his hand up to Margaid, he nodded at the admittance clerk.

"Very well, sir, tell me when you're ready."

"No, I don't mean you."

The lady shifted her eyes back and forth. "Of course, you didn't and how may I help you?"

"This girl right here needs some help."

The clerk's eyes arched, and she bore her gaze into Andrew. "She can't see me. I told you, no one can see me but you." He smiled at Margaid so she would know everything was all right, and then he turned back to the admittance clerk. "She says no one can see her."

Margaid's face puckered into a sucking lemons expression. "It smells in here."

The lady gazed at him with a blank stare and ignored Margaid.

With a shrug, he explained, "She says she's a lhiannan shee."

The clerk's eyebrows arched.

"Andrew, I don't like it here. I think we should leave." Gesturing Margaid to be quiet, he spoke louder to the clerk.

"She says the sea god

told her to drain men's blood into a red cauldron." "Andrew, they keep human blood here. I can smell it." "Ma'am, are you listening? Stop staring, my friend needs help."

"All right." The lady in blue scrubs crossed her arms over her chest. "Where is she?"

"How can she help me if she can't see me?" "Margaid, I can't talk to two people at once, please be quiet." He leaned closer to the clerk's window. "She's right here in front of you." He wrapped his arm around Margaid's shoulder.

"I see." The admittance clerk's lips grew tight, and her eyes narrowed. "And what is your name?"

"I'm Andrew Quayle, I'm an American."

The lady began typing on the computer. "Address please?" "Why are you giving her your address? You never gave me your address. Andrew, you don't even know this woman. I don't like the way she's looking at you."

"I don't like the way she's looking at me, either." He tilted his head toward the clerk. "I don't think you need my information, do you? You need Margaid's."

"Very well, stay right here, please." The slant of her eyes and the arch of her brows suggested she'd cast him aside. "A nurse will be with you soon." She picked up the phone and pushed a button. "We have a situation. We need someone up front."

"Andrew, I'm not a situation and neither are you. We should just leave if that's the way they're going to be."

"Margaid, the doctors here can help you. I'm sure of it." He inhaled slowly. "Just please be quiet."

"Why? They can't hear me."

Soon, a middle-aged woman in a white, zip-front tunic and straight-legged slacks stepped up to him. "Hello sir, come with me please." She led him into a small room with an examination table. She motioned to Andrew to sit on the table.

"Me or Margaid?"

"I'm not sitting down there, Andrew. I want to go back to my cave."

The nurse sat in the chair. "Margaid?" The nurse's forehead crinkled.

"Yes." Were these women blind? He pointed at Margaid. "Yes, that's me, the lhiannan shee."

The nurse kept her gaze on Andrew. "How can I help you?" "I brought Margaid, she's the patient." Was everyone on this island either dense or crazy?

"Is she here with us?" The nurse scanned the small office as if looking for Margaid.

"Of course I'm here with you. I'm not going to leave Andrew alone in this awful place. It smells like sickness in here." Margaid crossed her arms over her chest.

"Yes, she's speaking to you right now." What's wrong with this nurse?

"Sir, this may seem like a dumb question, but do you know that no one's here but you and me?"

"Are you crazy? She's right here."

Margaid's eyes widened. "Andrew, I think she thinks you're crazy."

"Why don't you tell me a little about Margaid?" The nurse leaned closer to him.

"I don't like this woman. Don't tell her anything about

me." "Look, I'm not crazy. She's here, but she says no one can see her but me. That can't be true. It makes no sense."

"Of course it makes sense, Andrew. It's part of the lhiannan shee lore because I'm your slave. I keep telling you that." "How long have you known her?"

"I just met her tonight. She lives under the sea. She says she's something called a lhiannan shee." He looked the nurse straight in the eye, hoping he could get her to understand. "I'm not crazy. It's true." He let out a sigh. "You really don't see her?"

Margaid stepped but a breath span from the woman and waved her hands in the nurse's face. "Hello, hello."

"I don't see anyone in here but you and me. However, did you say she's a lhiannan shee?"

Andrew chuckled at Margaid's antics. "That's what she says. I know it makes no sense, I never even heard of it before."

"You're not from the island."

"Does he sound like he's from the island?" Margaid rolled her eyes.

"No, I'm an American."

The clerk looked at him with a skeptical smile on her face. "How did you learn about the lhiannan shee?"

"Margaid told me."

"Lady, he knows all about the lhiannan shee. He has one as a slave."

The nurse closed her eyes for a moment. "She's with us now."

"Yes." Andrew and Margaid spoke simultaneously.

"Can you finally see her?"

"No, but I feel her energy. I'm Manx, I know of the lhiannan shee."

"You don't look like you know much to me," Margaid quipped.

"So you believe me." Andrew smiled with relief.

"Yes, but I don't know if I can help you. The lhiannan shee kill their prey."

"What did you say?" Margaid placed her hands on her hips. "I've never killed anyone. But I might make an exception and drink your blood."

"Margaid says she's my slave because I resisted her seduction."

"You tell her." Margaid's face flushed red with anger.

"What?" The nurse gulped. "She wasn't able to seduce you?"

"Look lady, that's none of your business." Margaid scowled.

"Well, I tied her hands, anyway, she couldn't complete the seduction." His cheeks felt hot with embarrassment. "So, it's as if I resisted her charms. That's what she says." He hoped this nurse didn't ask him anything else.

The nurse rubbed her forehead. "The lhiannan shee are unmatched in their beauty. They seduce men with their looks alone."

"Well, that is true." Margaid began to calm down.

"Well, I lost my contacts. So, she's as much a blur to me as you are."

"You can't see her well?"

"No."

"That explains it." The nurse leaned back in the straight wooden chair and laughed. "The lhiannan shee are fey. If you'd been able to truly see her, you couldn't resist her charms."

"Finally, she's beginning to understand." Margaid sighed.

"Are you saying if I had had my contacts, I'd be dead now, my blood drained into a big cauldron?"

"Yes, no matter how sweet this Margaid seems, you can't underestimate the lhiannan shee."

"Forget what I said, she doesn't know what she's talking about, Andrew."

"So, you think she's dangerous?"

"Andrew, how can you say that?" Margaid asked in a hurt tone.

"Well, you said she's your slave."

"Yes, that's what she says."

"Yes, I am."

"Then she's no danger to you now. But why do you want help? You won, you have a lhiannan shee enslaved to you."

"That's what I've been telling you, Andrew."

"Are you crazy? I'm an American. I can't bring an enslaved Manx, fairy-vampire home."

"Then it's not a hospital you need, it's a druid." The nurse stood.

"She might have something there."

"Really?" The mental ward nurse thinks I should see a druid.

"Do you know any?"

"I know where you can find one. The laws that direct the lhiannan shee can only be broken by the god who created them. Only Mannan beg mac y Leir can change Margaid's fate. But it's not without risk. The sea god won't be happy when he finds his lhiannan shee enslaved to a man from America."

"Andrew, she's right."

"Well, I am a Quayle also."

"He won't care," the nurse said.

"But you're saying that he can give Margaid her freedom."

"He is the only one who can, but before you go asking a trickster god like Mannan for a favor, stop and think for a moment. He can just as easily turn you over to a lhiannan shee who'll drink your blood. Margaid will be free, but you'll be dead. The chance of Mannan beg mac y Leir keeping both you and Margaid alive and free... is slim."

Andrew rubbed his forehead. "This is a crazy island with its four horned sheep, cats with no tails, and now this. It's all warped and fifth dimensional."

"You know, it's your choice." The nurse shrugged. "Leave matters as they are and learn to be happy, or have a druid summon Mannan at risk to your own life."

"That's scary." All this started just because I was looking for a club to go to.

"You have to sort it out. It's like that American expression—shit happens."

"Is that her medical opinion?" Margaid's brows arched.

"I guess so." Andrew rolled his shoulders in a shrug. "I don't even know how to find a druid."

"At the nearest metaphysical store, Celtic Cauldron, just two blocks down. Ask for the owner. If you're sure that's what you want to do." The nurse's tone held a hint of warning.

"Okay, can we go now?" Margaid headed to the door.

"Let's go back to my hotel. I have to think about this, and I need a drink or two."

"Me too." Margaid grabbed his hand.

He nodded at the nurse. "Thank you."

"Enjoy your stay on the Isle of Man."

"Sure." Everyone on this island is crazy. "I'm having so much fun. So glad I came."

As Andrew walked out, he overheard the admissions lady ask the nurse, "Are you going to just let him walk out, as mental as he is?"

"No, he's not crazy, just an American having a little joke on us."

"Well, as if I didn't have better things to do," quipped the woman in blue scrubs.

"Hurry," Andrew goaded Margaid.

CHAPTER 3

They walked as fast as they could away from Nobles Hospital. Andrew stopped in his tracks when he noticed the store they had just come to was the Celtic Cauldron.

Relief filled him when he read the closed sign on the door. *Good, I can't deal with this right now.* "We have to come back tomorrow."

"Andrew, I don't want some lhiannan shee drinking your blood. I won't be able to stand it. Why not keep things as they are?"

He gazed at her oval face. Even without his contacts her could make out her rounded, dimpled cheeks. His gaze fell to the shapely curve of her ample bust. His fingers itched to squeeze them, pinch them, his mouth moistened at the thought of sucking them.

"We'll talk about it soon." He wrapped his arm around her as they crossed the street. His skin tingled from the contact of her warm, soft skin. He pointed to the glitzy building on the seafront. "Here we are." Pressure coiled in his crotch, muscles clenching throughout his pelvis. His cock and testicles felt wrenched tight with desire for her.

"Wow, this is big. This is your house?"

"No," he laughed. "It's the Hilton." Nodding to the doorman, Andrew led her inside.

"I've heard people call it that. What's a Hilton, is it like a chief's house or a castle?" She swept her gaze over the spacious lobby.

"No, it's a place Americans go when their parents are paying for the vacation."

"I've also heard this place called a casino. What is that?" "It's a place you go to lose money."

"Why would anyone want to lose their riches?" She followed him down a short hall.

"Good question." Andrew led her to the elevator and pushed the button. When the doors opened, he motioned to her. "Come on in."

"It's so small."

"It's an elevator."

"I'm telling you, Andrew, it's too small." She stepped inside. "With a big estate like this Hilton, they should let you have a larger room."

He chuckled. His favorite thing about Margaid was the way she made him laugh. The elevator came to a stop, and the doors slid open. "Come on." He stepped out and gestured for her to follow.

"Where are you going? Why are you leaving? We just got here?"

"It took us up, so we didn't have to climb the stairs. This is our floor."

"Wow, its magic. It moved us." She followed him down the hall.

He swiped his card key at their room and as he held the door open for Margaid, he asked her, "Want something to eat?"

"Oh, yes. I can make yummy food for us, Manx kippers from herring and *Manx queenies* with scallops, and I can fix *bonnag* for dessert."

"Or I can just call room service." Hunger pulled his stomach tight and his lower pelvis area even tighter, but it wasn't food he craved. It was Margaid's silky skin and alluring curves. Still eating might take the edge off. "Want hamburgers? You eat, don't you?"

"Yes, I eat. We keep the blood in the cauldron for Mannan beg mac y Leir, like a sacrifice. We seldom drink it." Her face twisted into a 'that's disgusting' expression. "The taste is thick. It's hard to swallow. I can't remember the last time I drank blood." Her eyes grew rounder than usual. "I don't think I ever have." She sat down on the bed. "Wow, this is soft."

Then he noticed the suitcase at the foot of the bed. "My bag." Grabbing it, he pulled out his contacts. He ran to the bathroom and slipped them in. When he stepped back into the bedroom his breath caught in his throat with his first good look at Margaid. A surge of heat shot through him. His balls felt squeezed, and his erection hardened.

Her perfect oval face looked as luminous as an alabaster sculpture, with plump cheeks, dusted rose, and the added dazzle of a generous sprinkle of auburn freckles. He couldn't tear his gaze away. She parted her full lips, revealing pearly teeth. As he peered at her, his heart thudded.

She ran her fingers from her temple through the long red strands of hair which tumbled in graceful curves down her back. Revealing a dainty ear adorned with a large pearl, probably taken from an oyster from the sea bottom near her cave.

"You're not squinting anymore. Can you really see better with slips of glass over your eyes?"

He couldn't concentrate on what she was saying, he only knew a flaming sensation engulfed him with one good look at her. "You're gorgeous."

"I am?"

Covering her soft cheeks with his hands, he gazed into her eyes. He was a goner, drowning in her beauty. Tilting his head, he covered her mouth with his. He twisted his lips over hers, devouring the warm saltiness. Her trembling lips parted, and he plunged his tongue inside her mouth, flicking it in and out, plunging deeper each time. She let out soft, moaning sounds as he stroked her hot, wet mouth. Fully aroused, hard as iron, his erection twitched with need.

Andrew glided his hands from her cheeks to her smooth shoulders and shoved her onto the bed. With his fingers, he gathered the thin fabric of her chiton and peeled it off her. He gaped at her lush, rose-tipped breasts. She was magic all right.

He cupped a mound in each hand, squeezed and massaged the sultry flesh. Margaid's moans almost thrust him over the edge as he pinched the pebble hard tips. Leaning his head down, he captured a quivering nipple between his teeth and gently tugged. His tongue lashed the thrusting peak without mercy. Her breast jiggled, mesmerizing him all the more. A rush of heat swept through him. Margaid's breath grew shallow.

"You make me happy. I need you, want you inside me, so bad."

"Me too." Andrew's palms tingled from the heat of her

skin as he glided them across the flat of her belly and to the juncture of her thighs. "The whole vampires or lhiannan shee are real thing and you wanting to claw me to shreds has me freaking out. Nervous." His fingers explored the red whorls between her legs. "But I need you. Have to push into your softness." He slid his fingers down the downy nest to the stiff nub, and he flicked it.

Margaid's quick intake of breath turned into a high-pitched squeal.

"Plus, you make me laugh and there is no woman on earth as beautiful." Withdrawing his fingers from the entrance to her sex, he grabbed her thighs. With one hand on each, he slid her legs apart and gaped at the pink, moist prize his growing erection ached for. "I've got to have you now."

At that moment, there was a knock on the door. "Andrew, I'm coming in, okay?"

"What?" His breath was heavy, and he could barely speak. In his head, he screamed no.

What a nightmare for his mom to walk in on him now. He leapt off the bed and glanced at Margaid who lay there fully bared, with jutting breasts and arched thighs spread wide.

He tilted his head toward the tall, strawberry-blonde woman of average weight, who strode in wearing a white terry robe over blue pajamas. "Mom."

"You look so flushed." She peered straight at him as if she hadn't even seen Margaid. "I hope you're not coming down with anything."

I'm coming down with Margaid. "No, I feel fine." Okay, she can't see her. His gaze darted to the woman lying on his bed. Only I can see her. There he was, gaping again at her breasts. His eyes shifted to the quivering petal like folds between her legs where pure joy awaited him.

"Andrew, what's wrong? Why is your mouth hanging wide open as you stare at your bed? You must really be tired?"

"No, Mom, I'm fine."

"Did you see the bag?"

"Yes, Mama." He was afraid to ask, but he had to know for sure. "Do you see anyone else here?"

"Oh, you mean like a ghost as in the ghost of our ancestors?"

"Something like that." He felt like an idiot. "No, you're right, no one's here but me and you."

"Kiddo, don't make fun of me for coming all this way to find my roots." She ruffled his hair like she had done back when he really was a kid. "We're going to meet downstairs in the Paragon at 9:00 am, to take the train to Cregneash and see how people used to live."

"Where they live in huts with thatched roofs, plow with horses and spin and weave?"

"That's it. Oh, and be on your best behavior tomorrow, we're having company for breakfast."

You don't know the half of it. We're having company right now. "Sounds great." Andrew gaped at Margaid's wonderland. It would be a wild ride all night long. He could start as soon as he got his mother out of here. He smiled. "I'll be there."

His mother gave him a peck. "Good night." She closed the door behind her.

"She really can't see you."

"No, only you can." Margaid stressed the word 'you' in a

humorous tone.

He swept his gaze down her long, shapely legs to her arched thighs. "Unbelievable. True magic."

His palms still burned from the touch of her before his mother burst in.

"I don't know how long you'll feel that way. As your slave, I'll be with you for the rest of your life. You might get tired of looking at me."

"Never." He felt his soul melt when he peered into those emerald eyes.

She eased into a sitting position. "Of course, Mannan beg mac y Leir may draw that short, with one poof of his magic wand, I could be a water horse."

"I won't let him. And I could never grow tired of you. It's not possible." But you will. Tired that no one can see you but me and fed up with being my slave. "It's not right. It can't be. I have to find that druid to get that old sea god to set you free."

"Why don't you want me?" The sparkle in her eyes seemed to fade. "I mean, want me with you. I didn't kill you. I didn't drain your blood. I could never do that. I've never hurt anyone." Her voice was shaky. "Why do you want to get rid of me, even at risk to your life?"

As he gazed at her jutting breasts, the nipples still tight and erect from the earlier ministrations of his fingers and tongue, his throat went dry, and his breath grew shallow. He managed to speak, those it came out raspy. "Crazy, the last thing I want is to get rid of you." Plopping down on the bed at her side, he draped his arm around her waist. "You're incredible. It's not right for you to live an entire lifetime invisible to everyone but me, unable to speak to anyone but me or be with anyone but me. To not even have a friend. I couldn't do that to anyone. I certainly can't do it to the woman–" *I almost said it. Is it true? Is she's the woman I love?*

Do I love her? "It's not right for you, Margaid. We have to talk to the sea god."

Her eyes glittered with fear. "No."

She said it so loud he jumped, startled.

"He could kill you. I won't let you speak to him. So I'm your slave. I'm happy. I don't want to be someone else's slave and I don't want to take men's blood. I like you Andrew. I like being with you. I'm satisfied like this. If I can't be with you, I'd rather be a water horse."

"No." Andrew felt like she had unwittingly broken his heart. He couldn't lose her. She couldn't let the sea god turn her into anything. He wanted her.... needed her....loved her. "People can't belong to other people as slaves. I can't do that. I'd rather die than do that to you."

"So, you want to talk to Mannan beg mac y Leir?"

"Yes, we'll go see that druid."

"You talk to him then, because I don't want to." She mimicked the neighing sound of a horse. "Where are my oats and hay?"

"What?" He released a deep chuckle.

"I'm practicing being a *cabyll-ushtey*."

"I won't let him run his magic wand over you." He took her dainty chin in his fingers. "I promise. I like you just the way you are." Her warm breath fanned his face. He couldn't focus on water horses and Mannan beg mac y Leir, all he could think of was Margaid.

He tilted his head down until their lips touched. A fiery heat cut through him. His mouth devoured hers. The throbbing in his groin deepened. His cock hardened.

When he reluctantly drew his lips away, Margaid rasped, "Oh really, because speaking of magic wands–"

"Now, my wand is a different matter." His erection jerked

with the need to bury itself inside her soft, moist heat. "I very much want to run it over you."

She let out an exuberant whoop. "Let's take a peek."

Andrew drew in a sharp breath as Margaid pulled his zipper down. The brush of her fingers against his crotch almost had him undone.

"So big." Her eyes grew wider.

"Flattery is not needed. Believe me." She didn't need to do anything more to get him in the mood.

"He's such a big...boy."

"He's hot for you." Andrew fought the urgent need of his cock to push into her now.

"That I can see."

"He wants to come inside you."

"He grew big and hard just for me."

"Yes, it's all for you." He wouldn't be himself until he had her. He couldn't take his eyes off her, nor could he think of anything but Margaid. As she clutched his jeans at his hips and peeled off his pants, he gazed into her shiny, intense eyes.

"*Ta Graih aym orrym,*"she breathily whispered.

"What does that mean?"

"I love you." Her red lips stretched into a warm smile. Andrew gaped at her lips, so lush and full. "What did you say?"

"*Ta Graih aym orrym.*"

"Yeah. You could be telling me anything. You could be saying I'm a bad lay."

Her expression suddenly grew serious. "I love you," she said. "*Ommidjagh!*" Her voice held a bemused tone.

"And what is *ommidjagh*?" He gulped. Gosh, she was going to make him admit he loved her. The moment he'd put his contacts in, he knew he was a goner. "Does it mean sweetheart?"

"No, it means you're bad in bed." She flashed a wry smile. "Not funny."

"It means silly." She let out a soft chortle.

"Oh, I have to make you pay for that. I'll show you silly." His leaned his mouth toward her lips that tasted of heat and honey. The minute his mouth touched hers, he was on fire. When he slipped his lips off hers, before he could think, he told her, "I love you." Boy, was he in trouble.

Margaid returned his kiss with a hard smooch and tugged on his lower lip with hers. She eased her lips off his and met his gaze. "You shall be greatly rewarded. For you love me so much, you'll risk your life so I can be free."

"And what is my reward?" He leaned his head close to hers.

A smoldering promise of things to come gleamed in the depths of her eyes. She swung her leg over his, straddling him. He leaned his back against the soft bed. Tilting her head down to his bare sex, she slipped her fingers around the base of the hardened flesh. She parted her lips and took the mushroom head into her mouth.

With the intense, yet pleasant pressure in his groin, he closed his eyes, let out a deep moan. His cock sunk into her hot mouth. Then she slid her red lips back, until his erection lay almost fully exposed. As she stroked and suckled his tingling, burning flesh, his breathing came in pants. He felt his cock rub against the roof of her mouth, then touch the back of her throat. He gasped. She fluttered her soft fingertips on his ballocks in a circular motion.

His entire body shuddered. Between her skilled fingers and her mouth, he would burst at any moment.

"Margaid, I only want to come inside fire between your legs."

Drawing her mouth off him, she shifted her body, and her red whorls, nesting her soft sex, rubbed against his rock-hard cock. She guided his erect arousal inside her, burying it to the hilt. Wrapping his cock in the warm, wet silk of her tight sheath as it stretched to accommodate him.

She was so tight. He had to push into her again and again. His body would have nothing else. He thrust forward, and she bucked with the impact.

Margaid's soft gasps and whimpers inflamed him even more. He lunged deeper into her hidden heat. She rocked back and forth, riding him hard as he ground his iron flesh into her fiery, liquid core. In and out, he pumped his fire-brand into her, plunging deeper, higher, and faster each time.

Margaid panted and moaned. The hotel bed creaked to the rhythm of his thrusts. He was so relieved his mother's room was across the hall, if she'd been on the other side of that wall, she'd hear all their primeval noises as they made love.

He planted one palm on each of her breasts and squeezed her soft flesh hard. Her mouth dropped open and her red tongue darted in and out as she panted like a freight train. He flicked his thumbs against her nipples, and she whimpered with ecstasy. Desperate for release, her fierce cries of pleasure heated his blood. A surge of liquid heat flooded her tight passage, as he pumped into her, hovering on the edge of an explosion, until they quivered with release together.

His hammering heartbeat began to slow. Andrew's rushing huffs ebbed into normal breaths. Gently, she pulled off him and lay at his side.

He wrapped his arm around her soft flesh, glistening with perspiration. He rose on one elbow, leaned down, and kissed her trembling lips. Sucking the salty taste and breathing in the tangy scent of her sex.

He withdrew his mouth from hers and gazed down at Margaid as she lay by his side. Her lids slipped over her eyes and her face held a dreamy expression.

There was another knock. What now? "Mom?"

From the other side of the door, someone called, "Room service."

"It's the burgers and sodas." Having yanked his jeans back on, he opened the door, took the tray, and handed the guy a tip.

Soon, he and Margaid were devouring the greasy hamburgers.

"This is so yummy and delicious." Grasping the large bun as best she could, sauce dribbled down her chin as her meat slipped further out of the bun. She shook her glass. "What are these clear, cold pebbles?"

"Crushed ice."

It had been a long night. He gobbled down the hamburger, leaving nothing but a piece of lettuce on the plate. "I'm so sleepy now."

He gazed at Margaid, taking in her lush shape.

She reached down and wrapped her fingers around his cock.

Suddenly, he felt wide awake.

"You are so hot. You burn my fingers. Let me cool Mr. Big down." She dipped her long fingers deep into the cup and pulled them out, dripping wet and clutching a handful of crushed ice. She opened her lips wide and dropped the slippery pellets inside her mouth.

Straddling his thighs, she curled her fingers around the

base of his erection and took his cock into her mouth with the ice rolling around. The sensations of freezing and flaming had him moaning mercilessly.

She shifted her hand round his shaft as she moved her mouth up and down him. The ice and her mouth caused fiction, massaging his flesh, stroking every nerve. Cold and hot shivers racked his body. He panted mindlessly as he quivered in ecstasy.

She drew her mouth off his cock, tilted her head up, and gazed into his eyes. "Ice, you say. I like it."

He rasped, "Me too."

Before she could say anything, he grabbed her hips and rolled her over, so now his body was on top. "Your turn."

Andrew grabbed the cup and tilted it to his lips, filling his mouth with ice. He clamped his lips together till the crushed ice melted, leaving his tongue cold. He grasped her thighs and spread her legs till her she lay opened full before his gaze. He reached into the coke and pulled out one pebble of crushed ice and rolled it across the folds of her red flesh. Then he licked her delicate flesh with his icy tongue. She quivered and mewed.

He thrust his cold tongue in and out of her hot channel. until she bucked beneath him.

Then, he slipped his finger inside her pussy, pumping her. He reached for the cup and dipped his fingers in the crushed ice, then roamed his fingers across her breasts, pinching her nipples. He replaced his finger with his rock-hard cock, plunging into her.

His pleasure peaked. She clenched against his cock then he went over the edge in a blaze of heat. She mewed as he moaned. Their bodies quivered together.

"You're so hot." He pulled out and plopped down beside her. Exhausted.

She pulled the red Hilton spread over both of them. The moment she laid her head on the plump pillow, she fell asleep.

Andrew's eyes drank in her beauty. I hope I didn't put you to sleep. That our lovemaking bored you. Then he remembered it was the most passionate experience he'd ever had. No, that couldn't be it.

"*Ta Graih aym orrym,*" he whispered. What am I going to do? Why does this whole thing bother me so? Isn't it great, in a way? What every guy wants? An invisible, out of this world, gorgeous woman to serve my needs and desires. Should I try to find this druid or just go with the flow? This isn't such a bad thing, is it? Okay, I know. I'll make a list. Bad news first. I'll start with cons.

He exhaled. "Okay, first on the list, I might have to live in an underwater cave," he said aloud. "Second, no matter where I live, I'd have a red cauldron in the living room. A cauldron filled with blood. How will I explain that to friends and family who drop by?" Rubbing his chin, he continued talking to himself. "Third, if we have kids, they might be lhiannan shee and suck my blood. Fourth, my children might be invisible, lots of problems there. How will the doctor even deliver them? How will they go to school? If I'm the only one who can see them, everything might fall on me. I might have to deliver them. Okay, number four is really bad. Fifth, my father-in-law will be a sea god. What does a sea god do to a son-in-law he doesn't approve of? Okay, five is not good. Not good at all. Number six, there's an age difference, I'm 25, and she's thousands of years old. Okay, I'm going to quit the cons, it's getting scary."

"Okay, pros. Number one, she loves me. Two, she makes me laugh. Number three, great sex. Well, that's it, the pros have it."

"No, I can't keep her as a slave. I have to find Mannan beg mac y Leir and set this right. Even if it kills me, and the sea god may kill me, but there are worse things to die for than love or great sex. I'll go see that druid tomorrow and get this over with. Hopefully, Margaid and I can stay together."

On that thought, he shut his eyes and fell asleep.

CHAPTER 4

Andrew awoke to a banging on the door.

"Wake up, sleepy-head. Mom's waiting down-stairs. You were supposed to meet us. We're going sightseeing."

"Just a minute." He whispered to Margaid as she slowly opened her eyes, "It's my little brother." Andrew caught himself; he almost said 'you better put some clothes on.' "Are you sure he can't see you?"

"No one can see me but you, silly. I keep telling you that." "Okay, I just want to be sure."

"I'll stay under the covers until he's gone so you'll feel better." She stressed the word feel and gave him one of her adorable, goofy smiles.

The banging resumed. "Hold your horses, Mathew, I'm coming."

He pulled on his blue jeans, or rather some strange guy's jeans, and opened the door.

In walked a short version of Andrew, in appearance only, not in personality, as Andrew would gladly tell anyone who listened. No, Mathew was a major pain, all five feet of him. He swaggered in with his little eleven-year old self.

"What's up? What took you so long to open the door?" "I was asleep."

He flashed a toothy grin. "You've got a girl in here." "What?" Oh, no. "You can see her?"

"No. Don't be sarcastic. I don't see anyone. You've got her hidden. I can tell you've got a woman in here."

The little jerk. Andrew exhaled. "There's a girl in here, wow, thanks for letting me know."

"Ha, ha, ha, I'm serious. I know you."

Andrew glanced at Margaid sitting upon the bed with the covers pulled up to her shoulders. She was only eight feet from Mathew and staring right at him. The kid didn't have a clue. "Ha, ha ha, yourself." Andrew pulled out one of his shirts and buttoned it up. "Let me get dressed so I can meet Mom downstairs."

Mathew was stalking out the area around the bed. He made a sudden, dramatic move as if he thought he would find something and bent down to look under the bed.

He stood up again. A look of extreme disappointment etched his features. "Gosh."

"Disappointed?"

Then a huge grin filled his thin face, and he pounced on the floor on Margaid's side of the bed. He was a breath span from her face.

"Ah, ha." Mathew leapt back on his feet, his great catch clutched in his tight little fist. He held Margaid's chiton.

Andrew snapped his head toward her.

She shrugged. "He can't see or hear me and if my dress was on me, he wouldn't be able to see it, but since it's off, he can."

Andrew turned back to his little brother and said, "Look, knock it off. I need to get dressed now."

Andrew said the last word loudly, trying to tell Margaid to slip her clothes on.

Before the kid knew what had happened, Andrew snatched the chiton out of his hand and tossed it to Margaid. The moment she slipped it on, Mathew began blinking his eyes, staring at the air. Andrew could see she was fully dressed once more. But Mathew didn't see her at all.

"What happened? The dress flew up in the air and then it just disappeared."

"This is a lot to go through before breakfast." Andrew tugged his socks on.

Mathew just stood there with his mouth open. "Tell me about it."

Andrew looked at his brother's baffled face and chuckled. "If I didn't know better, I'd say you were drunk and seeing things."

"I wish." Mathew lolled his head to the side.

Andrew burst with laughter as he tied his tennis shoes. "There was no dress, little brother. Are you okay?"

"There was a dress. I had it in my hand. And I know there's a woman in here."

"I wish." Andrew flashed his brother a wide grin, then winked at Margaid.

"Oh no, don't tell me, I know. It's puberty isn't it? My rushing hormones made me imagine a woman's dress."

"I think so." Andrew was still laughing. The little sneak deserves it. Butting into my business. Trying to find my woman. Pesky little brother.

"You better hurry, then. Mom's downstairs and she's got a man with her."

"Oh, no." Andrew rubbed his forehead.

"Yeah. So, with her taste in men, he could be an axe murderer. We better get down there before he chops off her head."

Andrew turned to Margaid, and rolled his eyes toward the door so she would know to follow, though he remembered she told him as his slave, she had to go everywhere he did. As soon as they ate, he would find that druid and put an end to this. He only hoped it didn't put an end to him. And Mathew was right, his mother needed help when it came to men. Who would take care of her if something happened to him?

"Let's go," he said to Mathew and Margaid.

They took the elevator and strolled into the Paragon restaurant. Andrew spotted his mom sitting at a table by the glass wall, looking out at the sea. The man sat facing her, so his back was to Andrew.

"Let's go check this guy out." Andrew led the way over to his mom's table.

She smiled at them.

"Good morning, Mom." Andrew bent down and kissed her on the cheek.

The man shot up from his seat. "You."

Andrew's heart stopped for a moment.

"Those are my pants," the guy yelled.

"Oh, do you have a pair of jeans like Andrew's?" his mom

asked in a feigned cheerful voice, obviously trying to be nice until someone told her what was going on.

Just my luck. Andrew gaped at the same guy Margaid had stripped last night. "I can explain." But I really can't. Since no one in their right mind would believe me. Andrew felt sudden warmth as Margaid wrapped her arm around his shoulder.

"Why is he so mad?" Margaid looked confused. "I left him his boxers."

"I'm so sorry about last night and your clothes. I'll pay you for them." Andrew reached into his wallet.

His mother looked at him, "Andrew," then she glanced at her friend, "Bob, do you two know each other?"

"Yes," Bob said loudly as he stared at Andrew. "She's right, I know now. I know who you are."

Oh no, Andrew thought. The guy was probably going to call the police. After all, he had stolen Bob's clothes and stripped him naked except for his B is for Big shorts. Margaid did it, but the guy didn't know that, so now Andrew would end up in a Manx jail.

Mathew nodded at his mother. "I think they know each other."

"I figured it out." The man waved his finger. "You see, I thought about it all night and now I know who you are."

"I really didn't mean to steal your clothes. I didn't do it, really."

"Oh, you didn't do it yourself. You had one of your fey servants do it. It was probably a lhiannan shee."

"What is that?" his mom, Christine, asked.

"Leh noun she," Mathew said slowly.

"I never heard of it," Christine said.

"Actually, that's right. How did you know?" Andrew stepped closer to Bob.

"Oh, I know all about you. How you can transform into anyone. I know who you really are."

"I'm Andrew, Christine's son."

"No you're not. You're Mannan beg mac y Leir."

"Oh no." Had the whole world gone mad? "You have it all wrong." Andrew shook his head.

"Who's that?" Mathew's brows arched.

Andrew turned to his brother, who seemed the sanest person at the table at that moment, which in itself was a bad sign. *Boy, am I in trouble.* "Mannan beg mac y Leir's the sea god."

"Oh." Mathew turned his gaze on Bob. "So you've met my brother the sea god before?"

"Yes, last night, he worked his magic on me."

"Woo ho," Mathew said. "Geez, Andrew, I thought you liked girls."

"Shut up," he snapped at Mathew. "You're not helping at all."

Christine leaned back in her chair. "What's going on here?"

"Great news, Mom," Mathew quipped. "You finally found a man who will treat you like a goddess."

With a slight flutter of her lashes, Christine smiled coyly. "Oh, really." She let out a flirty giggle.

"You're the mother of a god, which makes you a goddess." Mathew stood, raised his arms high and with a dramatic flair animatedly bowed to his mom. "Hail the goddess, Christine, mother of the sea god."

"Stop that, Mathew," his mother scolded.

"Mighty god of the waters."

"Cut it out, Mathew." Andrew turned his head back to Bob.

"Look, I'm not the sea god."

Mathew bowed toward his older brother. "Praise the sea god."

Andrew wheeled around toward his little brother. "Stop. Now."

"No, you are." Bob pointed to Mathew. "He's right." Raising his tattooed arms high, he bowed to Andrew as well. "Praise mighty Mannan beg mac y Leir, god of the sea, god of transformation, the trickster god."

Andrew balled his hands into fists and knocked them together. "Please stop." He backed away, ready to leave.

"What is going on here?" Christine stood up. She grabbed hold of Mathew's arm and physically brought his bowing to a halt.

Still, Mathew flashed a bold smile. "Your date thinks Andrew is a sea god, and he's worshiping him."

Christine glanced at Bob, who was still bowing. "Good lord, I can't believe this. Why can't I find a normal man? What is wrong with me?"

"It's not you, Mom." Andrew tried to comfort her.

"I think you need to leave now," Christine told Bob. She reached into her purse, pulled out a credit card, and handed it to Andrew. "Get yourselves breakfast. I'll be in my room." She ran to the elevator, crying.

"Mom." Mathew hurried after her.

Andrew turned to Bob. "Here, let's go to the gift shop right now and I'll buy you some new clothes."

"No need. All I ask of the great Mannan beg mac y Leir is that you bless me with a prosperous year."

Whatever. Andrew just wanted Bob gone at this point. "You shall prosper in all ways. Your prayers are answered."

"Thank you, thank you." Bob backed out of the restaurant, bowing all the way.

Andrew took Margaid's hand. "Come on, let's go find that druid. I can't take much more of this."

He stopped by the front desk, placed the credit card in an envelope, and had the bellhop take it up to his mother.

Andrew and Margaid strolled out of the hotel onto the wide Victorian promenade.

Her long red hair streamed in the wind as they ran ahead of a horse-drawn tram and crossed the street to the sidewalk by the bay. He breathed in the strong, invigorating scents of salt and fish.

Today could be his last day on earth, if this god judged against him. "Is Mannan a good god?" He glanced at the Victorian hotels and well restored buildings they passed by.

"Well, he takes care of the sea and all its creatures." Margaid gazed at the sparkling blue water of Douglas Bay as she walked at Andrew's side, still clutching his hand.

"So, are you part of the sea?" Andrew turned his head to look at the bay. The water was so still, it almost looked like jade, stretching out forever with the sun glistening upon it.

"I'm a fey creature of the sea, like the water horses and the selkies."

"But they are sea creatures, you're not." They passed an Indian restaurant, and he walked on, almost reluctantly knowing they would soon reach the store and everything would change for better or worse.

"No, but I serve Mannan beg mac y Leir. He's more than a sea god, he's also the god of transformation, and he's quite a joker as well."

"Margaid, my life will soon be in the hands of the sea god." Trying to take his mind off all this madness, he took in the details of the grand buildings—straight white columns, the overhanging bay windows, sloping roofs, triangular gables, and small turret towers.

"It's all my fault. If I wasn't such a bad lhiannan shee, none of this would have happened." She brushed tears off her face with the flat of her palms.

"Margaid, no, it's not your fault. If you weren't so bad at

being a lhiannan shee, I'd be dead." Heat shot through him as her soft hand squeezed his. "No matter what, I'm glad everything worked out the way it did, or I never would have met you. Margaid, I have to talk to Mannan, it's the only chance you have for a normal life."

Tears streamed down her face. "Andrew, I love you."

"Oh Margaid." Wrapping his arms around her shoulders, which felt like warm satin, he pulled her close. Her admission of love heated his blood. He felt so much more than lust for this woman. Andrew wanted to protect and care for her. "This is it. We're at the shop." His breathing was so heavy, his heart throbbed. "I have to fix this whole lhiannan shee, Mannan thing." He pulled her tighter to him. "Let's go and see this god."

CHAPTER 5

Having crossed the wide promenade, they entered the Celtic Cauldron. The spicy and tangy scents of herbs and incense made his nose tingle. It was worse than the department stores where ladies squirted perfume on Christmas shoppers.

A man in a long robe stepped out from behind the counter. He had long silvery hair, which curled on the ends and was tied back in a ponytail. Andrew gazed at the blue tattoos covering his arm, a crane drawn with Celtic tracery, a triskelion, swirls that looked like ocean waves, and one of an eye shaped like a fish with a fish's tail on the end. That's the same kind of tattoo the 'B is for Big' guy had. But it wasn't the same man. The shop owner's hair was gray instead of brown and he was older and taller. He appeared friendlier, his smile was broad and contagious, and his large eyes sparkled. Though elderly, his back was straight, and he stood with his hands on his hips, looking notably self-assured.

"Moghrey Mie." The shop owner gazed straight at Margaid.

Andrew recognized the Manx greeting. "Good morning to you as well, *moghrey mie*. You're smiling at Margaid, can you see her?"

"No, but I see an aura hanging in the air as if it surrounds a spirit and I feel energy, feminine energy."

"That's Margaid all right, feminine energy."

Margaid grinned at Andrew. "This man's the druid the nurse spoke of."

"Is she a spirit?" the druid asked.

"She's a lhiannan shee." Andrew's gaze met Margaid's, and he winked at her. It won't be long now. If this works out, she'll soon be free, but still with me. Hopefully.

The druid's brows arched in a puzzled expression. "Enslaved to you...you resisted her charms."

"Well, you see, I lost my contacts, so I couldn't see her that well, also I took her by surprise and seduced her before she could seduce me. You might say."

The elder man's luminous eyes widened as he gazed at Andrew. "That's quite a story."

"It's been quite an experience." Andrew stepped closer to him. "Can you help us?"

"Help?" The druid stared at Margaid and smiled. "What kind of help do you want?"

Andrew wondered if somehow the man really could see her. He had the oddest feeling about this. "I want Margaid free from slavery to me, so others can see her and she can decide for herself who she wants to be with, me or someone else. It's only right. She's a great person, she deserves freedom. Who doesn't? But Margaid is like a butterfly, a bird, she has to be free."

"What can I do?" The man's eyes gleamed.

"I am told you are a druid and you can invoke the god

Mannan beg mac y Leir. Only he can release Margaid from her vow of slavery to me."

"But you are a non-believer." The druid gazed at him with those piercing blue eyes, challenging him.

"I believe in Margaid. I can see and hear her. And I believe Mannan can make her human so we can be together, if that's what she wishes. It's our only chance at happiness. I want no other woman, only Margaid. She is my future."

"Mannan can be like a storm rising off the ocean, such is his temper, and he may not take well to your request," the druid warned.

Andrew nodded. "I have been told of the risk."

"I can perform a ritual. But once I start, there is no turning back. Are you sure you want to do this?" the druid asked.

"Yes." Andrew gazed into Margaid's smiling eyes as he took her hand in his and squeezed it. "I have to do this. You are not meant to be a slave."

"I want to be with you in whatever way I can."

"Margaid, if you love me, let me do this. I need to."

"I do love you and I can't talk you out of this. So, I'll stand by your side as you speak with Mannan beg mac y Leir."

"Very well," the shop owner let out a long sigh, "come into the back of the store, I have a small temple there."

Andrew clutched Margaid's petal soft hand, squeezing it as they walked together, following the man into a back room.

The druid gestured. "Margaid, you sit here, and Andrew, you sit there, facing each other." He sat a fat candle on the center of the table and lit it. "Reach across the table and grasp each other's hands." He raised his arms in the air.

Andrew reached out to stop him. "First, shouldn't we introduce ourselves? My name is Andrew, and you know of Margaid." Again Andrew noticed the druid smiling at Margaid. He swore he could see her. "And what's your name?"

"My name is...well, they call me Orbsen mac Alloid."

"Orbsen, I'm glad to meet you." He shook the druid's hand. Andrew almost yelled ouch. The old man had a surprisingly strong grip for his age.

Margaid grabbed Andrew's shoulder and he tilted his head toward her, but she didn't say anything. Her face was red, tense, and lined. The nails of her hand pressed against his skin. She stood up and pointed at the druid, then swung her head back to Andrew. Trying to tell him something important, her lips moved, but she didn't utter a sound.

"What's wrong?" Something's not right. "We have to go." He shot up out of his seat, but Margaid shook her head no. "I mean we'll stay." Andrew looked at Margaid, who now bobbed her head up and down. She wanted to stay, but something was off. "Okay, we'll stay."

He shifted his gaze back to Orbsen and shrugged to hide his confusion. "Shouldn't I pay you first?"

"No, not me." The druid remained calm in his expression and tone as he still sat in the wooden chair. "The god will ask for a sacrifice. Sometimes he wants it in a golden bauble or a sword, but other times he will ask for much more."

Andrew gulped, knowing he could easily be dead, drained of his blood at the hands of the god himself or another lhiannan shee. Margaid squeezed his hand tight, but she no longer dug her nails into him and her face was less lined. She was more relaxed, yet still unable to speak. He had to fight through the gamut of confusion, fear, anxiety, excitement, curiosity, and love for Margaid. As she sat back down, so did he.

Andrew nodded to the druid to begin.

Orbsen mac Alloid scooted his chair back, and with one fluid movement he stood. He lifted his hands into the air, waving them in a circular motion. Suddenly, the air sparked, and an amber light circled Orbsen. He transformed before Margaid and Andrew into a luminescent figure wearing a pale blue tunic, with a silver belt covered in knot work, and a darker blue cloak adorned with silver swirls. It was pinned with a large, penannular brooch.

Margaid gulped. "Why did you take my voice away?" She gazed accusingly at the druid.

"Because sometimes you speak too much. Still, I will hear what you ask of me and I will consider your request based on the service you have given me."

"What are you talking about?" Andrew whipped his neck toward the druid. "Who are you?"

"It's him." Margaid let go of Andrew's hand, clasped her palms together and stepped forward to Orbsen. "I failed as a lhiannan shee."

"You didn't find a man to seduce?"

"No, I found one, but he seduced me and now I'm his slave." Andrew tried to stay calm, but he wanted to grab Margaid's hand and run as fast as he could.

"It is good you have come to me." The glowing god with long silvery hair held out his hands to Margaid. "I will help you. I will slay him, so you will be free to seduce a man who cannot resist you."

"No, no, don't do that." She waved her hands in front of the god's face. "I don't mind being his slave. I want to be with him."

Andrew looked the god straight in the eye. "We love

each other and you can't change that."

The sea god ignored him and peered at Margaid. "What?" His brows arched and his glowing eyes widened. "He must be quite a man."

"Oh, he is." Margaid stood up and moved behind Andrew, who stood as well. She wrapped her arms around his shoulders and chest. "Here he is, his name is Andrew."

Andrew turned his head and gently placed a whispery kiss on Margaid's soft cheek. Then he turned his gaze back to the deity. "You are a trickster god aren't you? I am not afraid of you, and I won't let you hurt Margaid. I'll have you know, she is not a failure. She is the most wonderful lhiannan shee and the greatest woman I've ever met."

Mannon's lips turned up into a broad smile and he nodded at Margaid. "It doesn't sound like he resisted your charms. It sounds like you enchant him."

"Well, I don't have his blood in my red cauldron."

"I can see that." For the first time, Mannon peered at Andrew. "Your blood is still inside you, right?"

"Yes, no one drained my blood and I plan to keep it that way."

The god chuckled warmly. "Well, I can understand why you would prefer that."

"But I also want Margaid free. She deserves more than to live her entire life as my slave, and I won't let you turn her into a water horse either."

"Oh, I was looking forward to turning you into a *cabyll-ushtey*, Margaid."

"I wish you wouldn't. But if changing me into a water horse will keep Andrew safe, I would willingly become one."

Mannon raised his huge cape up. "If I flap this cloak between you, the two of you will forget each other forever."

"God Mannan beg mac y Leir, if it means he will still live, then do it. I don't want him harmed just because he wants me free."

The god chuckled and let go of his cloak, so the hem hit the floor.

Andrew quivered. Mannan beg mac y Leir seemed so cruel, actually laughing at them. If only he didn't harm Margaid, then Andrew could live with whatever the god dished out to him.

"Let's run through this again. Andrew, you want Margaid to be free, not a slave to you and not a lhiannan shee to me. A free, human woman. And you are willing to die to ask the favor for her." Then the god turned to Margaid. "You want Andrew to be kept safe and unharmed and you are willing to let me turn you into a *cabyll-ushtey*, which is in truth your greatest fear."

Andrew gazed into Margaid's eyes and they both answered yes.

The god's brow furrowed. "So, you would sacrifice yourselves for each other."

Andrew placed his hand gently on Margaid's shoulder and leaned down to her. "You shouldn't do that. I couldn't stand it if anything happened to you."

"Nor I you. The worst he will do to me is turn me into a water horse. I would rather that than to see you killed or harmed."

Mannon bellowed, "Why would you do this? Why sacrifice yourselves?" He turned to Andrew. "She's a lhiannan shee, who tried to drain your blood." He glared at Margaid. "He's an American tourist who tried to commit you to a mental hospital."

"She couldn't help it."

"He didn't mean to."

"You are both daft." The god shook his head.

"I love him."

"I love her."

"Oh love. You love each other," the sea god said with disdain.

"Don't hurt her." Andrew pulled Margaid behind him to protect her.

But she jumped out in front of him. "No, do whatever you want with me. You can change me into a water horse, you can change me into a barnacle, but let Andrew go."

Silence descended as Mannan lifted his spear. Just as fast as he raised his weapon, he dropped it to his side in a stance of peace and he burst out in a deep, warm chuckle. "Why would I harm either of you? I have nothing against love. I just wanted to see if it was true. Honestly, I have never seen a worse case of true love."

Mannan grasped the hilt of the magic sword hanging from his belt and withdrew the long, gleaming blade. He held it high and chanted. "Without delay, for love's sake, I, the god of the sea, transform this fey to a mortal woman. In darkness and light, now and forever, so it shall be."

A ray of golden light burst into the air, surrounding the long sword like a halo. "By the righteousness of my blade, Fragarach, you are free from the fey bonds and life of the lhiannan shee. You're human, Margaid."

———

Heat filled her body from her heart to her belly and radiated outward to her skin. A rapt joy bubbled in the core of her being. From the tips of her toes and fingers, the sensation of transformation deepened until she could barely stand.

Margaid reached out to steady herself as she staggered. She started to fall.

Andrew caught her with both hands on her waist. A mystifying tremor coursed through her body. Then it all stopped. Her heart fluttered. She slowed her huffing and caught her breath. This was it, the most profound moment of her long life. "I am human."

Gazing at her patron god, warm joy bubbled in her. "God of the sea, I give thanks to you for granting my wish. Blessings upon you, great god, Mannan beg mac y Leir." But how can I repay him? Is he not the most wonderful god? "I am sorry I failed you as a lhiannan shee."

"You didn't. I wait for my lhiannan shee to come out of their caves under the sea and find a man to seduce. When they do, they fall in love." Joy shined in his eyes and the warmth of his smile echoed in his lilting, majestic voice. "Margaid, I am known as the trickster god and rightly so, for I do love a good joke. And my lhiannan shee are a good joke on me. None of them have the spirit for seducing men or shedding blood. Take your rightful form as a mortal, for it fits your spirit best. And be off with your true love."

"Yes, yes, thank you. Yeah!" She wrapped her arms around Andrew. "Now I can truly be your lover. As a free woman, I choose to stay with you forever." People can see me and talk to me. I don't have to fill a red cauldron with blood." Bubbly laugher flowed from her. "I can throw the cauldron out."

"By the way, I'll need my red cauldron back." Mannon folded his arms across his chest.

Andrew's gleaming eyes widened. "Margaid, you're human!" His smile broadened. "And you choose to stay with me."

"Forever," she whispered. Then she let out a squeal of

happiness. "I am human, and you are human and we are together, whoop, whoop, de do."

She breathed in his musky outdoor scent and enjoyed the feel of his muscular shoulders beneath her hands.

She leaned her face to his and pressed feathery light pecks against his firm chin, each sculptured cheek, and his smooth forehead. Everywhere but his lips. With the tip of her tongue, she traced the outline of his lips. Her hunger to cover his mouth with hers grew until she almost wanted to scream. Still, she held back. She puckered her lips and pushed them against his in a fast smooch. She then scraped her teeth against his lower lip and drew away, leaning her head back. He grabbed her hair and yanked her head to his. Crushing her lips with his. He twisted his mouth over hers, and forced her lips open with a thrust of his tongue. Margaid moaned and shivered with desire as he stroked her mouth with his pliable tongue. She met his fervor as her tongue twined together with his.

Margaid heard someone enter the room, but wasn't about to let anyone or anything interrupt this kiss.

"Hello," somebody called.

A lady cleared her throat as loudly as possible until Andrew withdrew his mouth from Margaid's and turned his head. "Hello, you're the nurse from the hospital." Andrew's brow crinkled and his eyebrows arched.

What is she doing here? Margaid glared at the nurse. "She's more than a nurse." Mannan flashed a wry grin. The nurse gave a slight shrug. "I'm a druidess as well." "High priestess to Mannan beg mac y Leir," the god announced.

"Margaid's human now," Andrew told the druidess, then turned his gaze back to Margaid and made love to her with his eyes.

"I knew it would all work out." The nurse walked over to

them. "Mannan beg mac y Leir is a trickster, his rage can be as wild as a storm, but love doesn't anger him, except when someone steals his lover away."

Mannan held his palms up. "Don't bring up Fand."

"Well, though your wife left you once, she came back, and that says a lot." The nurse-druidess smiled sweetly at her patron god.

While the god and the druidess talked to each other, Margaid leaned up on her tiptoes and pressed her lips, still swollen and tingling from the previous kiss, against Andrew's.

He slid his hand down her dress to the bulge of her breasts. Her knees trembled. Even with the barrier of the fabric, she felt the sultry heat of his palm. She felt her nipples tighten until they were erect. She was on fire. Heightening the kiss, he tugged gently on her lower lip with his teeth, nibbling until she moaned.

Andrew pulled Margaid to him, crushing her against his rock-hard body. He slipped his warm tongue between her parted lips, as she dug her nails into his shoulders. Margaid felt like melted wax pooled into liquid heat at the base of a long, thick, flaming candle that never burned out.

The nurse-druid begged for their attention by clearing her throat as loudly as possible.

Margaid wanted to hit her. Why is she here? Doesn't she have better things to do?

Andrew eased his mouth away from Margaid's and they both turned toward the obnoxious noise.

"Go back to the hospital," Margaid told her.

The nurse-druidess' laugher rippled through the air. "So it all worked out and you are going to get married now." Her mouth curved into a friendly smile.

"Why not?" Andrew gulped. He bent down on one knee.

"I don't have a ring for you yet, but I'll get you one. For now, though, all I can do is ask. Margaid, will you marry me?"

Flooded with joy, ready to burst free of earth and float to the sky, her throat tightened, and her eyes welled up until she couldn't speak. This time, at least, she knew it wasn't because of Mannan's enchantment.

After taking a slow, deep breath, she squeaked out, "Yes, I will." Tears slid down her cheeks.

"I can perform the ceremony." Mannan beg mac y Leir beamed even brighter.

"Now?" Margaid gazed into Andrew's eyes. "You want to marry me now? But I don't have a cake or flowers or a silk and satin gown." What am I saying? I should have stopped at yes.

"Yes, now." Andrew's face beamed like the summer sun. "Why not?"

Margaid shrugged. "There's no reason not to. We'll get a cake later." She wanted to scream and yell with joy.

"I'll change things around." Mannan conjured up enough white roses to fill the room.

The nurse-druidess pulled two gold-speckled, white robes out of the closet and handed one each to Margaid and Andrew.

"I forgot, the father of the bride's supposed to pay for the wedding and Mannan beg mac y Leir, you owe me for all you put me through, so where is my cake?"

"Margaid, you'll get fat." Mannan winked. "Cake now," Margaid commanded the god. "Chocolate?" he meekly asked.

"Of course." She nodded.

An eight-layer tier cake, taller than Margaid, suddenly appeared.

Andrew looked scared. "I can't eat all that."

"I can," Margaid smugly announced, as she licked her lips. "It is Belgian?" She glanced sideways at the god.

"Of course, Margaid." He sounded hurt. "I would never proffer a faithful servant less than the best. Made just this morn by descendants of the ancient Belgae tribe, worshipers of mine. They created the delectable masterpiece as an offering to me and trust me, you don't even want to know the blessing they are asking for."

"Don't tell us." Andrew rolled his eyes. "I really don't want to know. I just want to marry Margaid." With a quick smack, he planted a warm, wet kiss on her plump lips.

"Let's get on with the wedding."

As he stood in his robe, waiting for the nurse-druid to finish braiding white roses in Margaid's hair to go with her milk-toned, gold speckled robe, he asked the god, "Why are the lhiannan shee different from other vampires, they don't drink blood, just drain it into red cauldrons?"

Mannan laughed. "My lhiannan shee love chocolate. They can't stand the taste of blood. So I have them keep it in a red cauldron. Pretty funny, don't you think? And even so, they never take any blood. It's just not their way. Their cauldrons are always empty."

"So they're vampires who don't drain or drink blood." Andrew scratched his head.

"Hilarious, don't you think?"

"Yes." Andrew chuckled.

"I love a good joke." Mannan grinned.

The nurse-druid brought a box of crystals in from the storeroom and laid them in a large circle on the floor. She tossed white rose petals inside the circle.

Andrew clasped Margaid's hand so their wrists touched in promenade fashion. "You're so beautiful."

He led her around the crystal ring, then they strolled into it, together.

Mannan stepped inside the center of the circle along with the nurse-druid. He gazed at Margaid and Andrew. "In the world of humans and the land of the fey, nothing can stand between a man and a woman meant for each other."

Andrew flashed a bright smile at Margaid as he squeezed her hand.

She peered deep into his blue eyes. "You want to marry me, spend your whole life with me?"

"Margaid, as in the famous American movie, you had me at hello or rather *Laa mie.*"

"You mean the moment I swam up to the docks, and you didn't have your contacts, and you could barely see me?"

"Yes, even without my contacts, I followed you to the bottom of the sea and into a magic cave, didn't I?"

"That you did." She rose on her tip-toes and brushed her lips across his cheek.

"And I've followed you every moment after that. I knew you were mine the minute I laid eyes on you as you walked out of the Hilton."

His lips touched hers like a whisper.

In a melodic voice, Mannan asked, "Fairest Margaid, do you take this man from this day forth, in weal and woe, forever and anon?"

"I do."

At Andrew's compelling smile, swirls of heat spiraled through her.

He didn't even glance at Mannan, he kept his eyes glued to Margaid.

"Andrew, do you plight your troth to this woman as her lover and protector, whether weal or woe, forever and anon?"

He rasped, "Yes, I do."

The fire that flickered in Andrew's eyes was so intense, Margaid fanned herself with

her hand.

Mannan withdrew his blade, Fragarach, again and laid it on the floor. "By leaping over the magic sword, you both cut ties with your life before this day."

Holding Andrew's hand, Margaid jumped with him over the blade.

The nurse-druidess and Mannan cheered loudly.

Andrew gathered Margaid into his arms and captured her mouth with his. A warm shiver ran through her.

When he pulled his lips off hers, Andrew smiled at the god Mannan. "When you leave us, and the druid Orbsen mac Alloid finds we are not only in one piece but married, he'll be surprised."

"No, Andrew, Mannan is Orbsen mac Alloid." Margaid flashed a bemused smile.

"Orbsen mac Alloid's his human name and cover. As soon as he said his name, I knew. That's why he took my voice away, so I couldn't tell you." She raised her shoulders. "I tried to."

Andrew turned to the god and laughed. "You had me going there for a moment."

Margaid giggled. "Such a joker." She patted the god on the back.

"Yes, indeed." Mannan grinned. "And what else am I?"

"God of the sea," she answered confidently, though she wondered why he asked.

"And?" Mannan folded his arms across his broad chest.

Margaid scraped her teeth across her lower lip. "Umm, the trickster god." What is he after?

Mannan sighed. "And?"

"And what?" Well, there's only one choice left that I can think of. "The god of transformation."

Mannan snapped his fingers. "That's it."

With a loud crack and a puff of smoke, he suddenly vanished and the 'B is for Big' boxers guy stood in his place.

"The tattoos...I should have known." Andrew slapped the heel of his hand against his forehead.

Margaid couldn't stop laughing. "I didn't know. I didn't even guess. Oh Mannan, that was a good one."

When his laughter subsided, Andrew asked, "So Orbsen or Mannan, my mom can see Margaid now?"

"Yes, everyone can. She's completely human." "Everyone," Margaid piped. "Everyone can see me." "Margaid, my mom has to meet you. We've got to tell her the good news. I think 9:00 am tomorrow will be good. Her flight leaves at 9:30 am."

"But then she won't have any time to get to know me."

"And no time to try to change my mind about staying here in Man with my new wife."

"You want to stay in Man? I can't believe it. How wonderful! Gosh, I've lived here for thousands of years. It's the only home I've ever had, though it's changed a lot over time."

"This place is wild and magical and it's your home. And I haven't had a chance to eat your kippers, queenies, or *bonnag* yet." He pulled her into the circle of his arms. "Yes, I want to stay here. It's the perfect place to live." He twirled her about.

She stopped giggling and gazed deep into his eyes. "Do you really think your mom won't like me?" You only want me to see her for thirty minutes. What does that mean?

"It's not you. How can anyone help but love you? No, she won't like the idea of all of this. More than that, she'll be hopping mad. Believe me, we won't get off as easy with my mom as we did with Mannan beg mac y Leir."

"Is she mean?" Margaid crossed her arms. "She seemed nice in your hotel room and at breakfast. Mannan liked her. And she liked him. They were dating, remember?"

"I think that was just a joke on Mannan's part."

"She's your mother. Shouldn't she have been at your wedding? And what about your little brother, don't you want him to get to know me?"

"I do, but it's a lot for them to take in. I didn't even know we were getting married until that nurse said so."

"You're not saying you're sorry you married me, are you?" "Never. But it's going to be a shock to my mom."

"That's why you have to give her some time to adjust to the idea. Introduce me to her. We don't have to tell her we're married or that you're staying here forever. Not right now. Try to persuade her to extend her vacation. That's all."

"Why not? Anything for you. I'm not sure that druid wedding is legal anyway, even though it was performed by a god."

"Andrew, don't tell her the sea god married us, she may not be ready for that."

"No." He let out a soft chortle. "She might take both of us down to Nobles Hospital."

"Gosh, I have a husband and a mother-in-law. A whole new family. I have to get her a gift."

"Buy anything you want."

"Goodie, I get to go shopping." Margaid clapped her hands. "While you pick out something for my mom, I'll get your wedding gift."

"Ah, you're so sweet."

"Mannan," the nurse said in a scolding tone.

"Oh, okay, Andrew your gift to Margaid is on the house,

complimentary. Free. Get anything you want, why not?" The large god shrugged.

"Can I get his mother's gift here also?"

"Both gifts are on the house. What is a god for?"

"I know, I'll buy her a gift and I'll also bake her some kippers. Then at least she'll know I can cook for you."

"She'll like that." He pressed his lips to hers. "Umm, let's get back to the hotel for our wedding night."

"Sounds good to me." A hot ache burned through her at the thought of his body entwined with hers.

ABOUT THE AUTHOR

When Cornelia Amiri was five years old, she saw Walt Disney's **The Sword and the Stone** and has been interested in Celtic history and mythology ever since and has written 40+ sci-fi fantasy romance books. She lives in sultry Houston, Texas with her muse, Severus the cat.

DANCE OF THE VAMPIRES
EXCERPT

For More of Cornelia Amiri's Vampiric Fey, The Dancing Vampire series is available now in eBook formats from All Romance Ebooks

The first book in the series is:

Dance of The Vampires

Seven vampiric temptresses dance with seven handsome highlanders. Then they turn on the men.

Ian captures Sorcha, giving his brothers a chance to escape.

With the vampiric fey woman still in his grasp, Ian is saved by the rising sun.

Sorcha's sisters vanish with the light of dawn leaving her trapped in the mortal realm.

Ian is bewitched by the wild delights she offers, and Sorcha can't resist the urges he stirs in her.

But her wicked sisters and his highland brothers only want to attack and kill each other.

Will Sorcha and Ian's sizzling passion prove strong enough to overcome the differences between human and fey?

Dance Of The Vampires, Excerpt:

Ian wobbled out the door of the pub ahead of his six brothers. Focusing as hard as he could, pushing one foot in front of the other, he stumbled across a field in the moonlight. A clump of gorse and heather brushed against his jeans.

"Brother, be careful not to step on a thistle in the dark," Lachlan yelled in slurred speech.

"I have my boots on," Ian snapped.

"Are you sure, little brother?" Malcolm, the oldest, called out. "You usually run barefoot and cry like a girl when you get a thorn in your foot."

"I was five years old the last time that happened." Tired of the lot of them, he stomped ahead. "I'd go off by myself and leave all of you here, but someone has to lead you home."

Well past midnight, silence engulfed the field until Calin burst out laughing and couldn't stop.

"Shut up," Angus, the middle brother, yelled.

"He's hammered." Errol nodded his head toward him. "He cannot help it."

"Well, I do not know what's so funny or why we had to leave right when I spotted the pretty women in the pub."

Tavish kicked a stone with his foot as he tromped through the grass with his brothers.

"Because we are all drunk." Lachlan's body wavered, leaning forward then back. "That is why the lassies started looking so bonny to you. Those were the same ones you called old and ugly when they first came in, you bampot."

"They were old, that was Liam's mother and aunt." Angus grabbed Tavish's head and jostled it back and forth. He ducked out of Angus' way.

"Ooch!" Ian jumped back.

"What is wrong with you?" Malcolm set his hand on his hip. Ian pointed to the ancient mound of stones caked over with

dirt and grass. "I almost stepped on a fairy mound." His stomach knotted.

"Brother, are you afraid of a pile of old stones?" Calin threw his head back and rocked with laughter.

"It's a cairn." Ian's heart still thudded from the near miss. "Any who disturb it will be cursed."

"I dare you to knock it over." Errol crossed his arms over his chest.

Ian stepped back, a horrified look on his handsome face. "I will not."

"I will." With long, sure strides, Tavish stepped toward the ancient gravesite.

"Do not do it." Ian's belly clenched even tighter, until he felt sharp jabs of pain.

Before the other six could stop him, Tavish drew back his foot and crashed it into the sacred cairn with a hard kick. A loud, sharp gasp from each of his brothers hung in the air. One lone stone rolled free of the mound.

Malcolm's mouth dropped open. "You disturbed the fey."

"You've done it now." Lachlan stepped back, attempting to separate himself from the sacrilege.

"He dared me." Tavish pointed at Errol. "I had to do it, now didn't I?"

"Errol's a turnip-headed bampot," Calin shouted. "You too, Tavish."

"I do not like it." Ian shook his head. "It's sacred. It's cursed." The knot in his stomach froze, growing as cold as ice.

"This is bad." Angus shook his head.

"Let's keep walking." Calin slid his foot forward with a confident stride.

Malcolm bobbed his head. "We should hurry home before something happens."

"We are," Errol snapped. "We're in this field taking a shortcut, remember?"

"Come on." Malcolm headed away from the disturbed monument. "Walk faster." He took the lead as the others followed.

"Look." Ian came to an abrupt stop.

His brothers froze as their gazes turned to where he pointed his finger. Seven women, all in odd dresses of green tartan silk, stood beside the cairn. Their lush, scarlet lips curved into smiles as seductive as warm kisses.

The Dancng Vampire Series is for ages 18 and up, only.

ALSO BY CORNELIA AMIRI

Code of Love

Code of Misconduct

Code Name Love

Hostage

Moonless Night

Druids In The Mist

The Warrior and the Druidess

Moon Goddess Wife

Timeless Voyage

The Celtic Fox

The Celtic Vixen

The Scottish Selkie

Queen Of Kings

Back To The One I Love

Peace Love Music

A Fine Cauldron Of Fish

The Wolf And The Druidess

The Dragon And the Druidess

The Bear and the Druides

The Unicorn And the Druidess

Pendragon's Obsession

The Lynx and the Druidess

To Love A London Ghost

The Ghost Lights of Marfa

Starry Conquest

As Timeless As Magic

As Timeless As Stone

The Brass Octopus

I Love You More

Forged of Irish Bronze and Iron

Reach

A Boomer Chick's Bingo Card

Love AI Style - Bundle

Swords and Roses - Bundle

Warrior Hearts – Bundle

Need Fire - box set

Dancing Vampires - Box Set

Druidry and the Beast – full series

STAY IN TOUCH!

Get your eBook autographed <u>here</u>.

Please visit my <u>facebook page</u>, my <u>twitter</u> and my <u>pinterest</u>.

I can be contacted via email and always appreciate feedback or comments about my books. <u>Email</u>

The latest information about my books and more can be found on my web site:
   http://CorneliaAmiri.com